CLICK

YEARS ON THE TEAM: 5

CATCHPHRASE: Groove and prove!

FAVORITE ACCESSORY: Rainbow stickers

BUSTER

YEARS ON THE TEAM: 0

CATCHPHRASE: Blurrrrp!

FAVORITE ACCESSORY: Hat

NEW YORK TIMES BESTSELLING AUTHOR
DALE EARNHARDT JR.
NASCAR HALL OF FAMER

BUSTER'S TRIP TO VICTORY LANE

Illustrated by
ELA SMIETANKA

An Imprint of Thomas Nelson

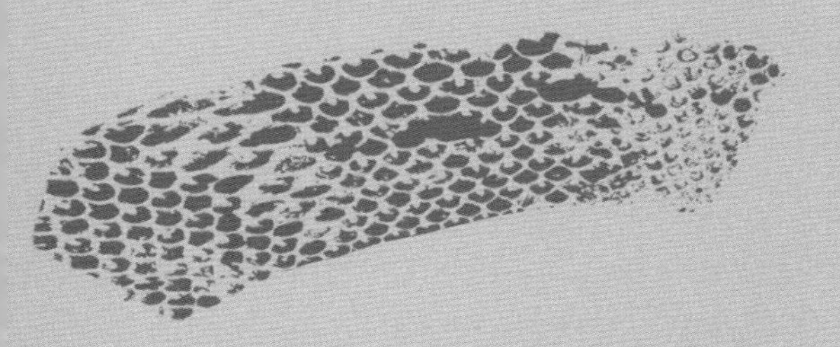

Buster's Trip to Victory Lane

Tommy Nelson, PO Box 141000, Nashville, TN 37214

Published in Nashville, Tennessee, by Tommy Nelson. Tommy Nelson is an imprint of Thomas Nelson. Thomas Nelson is a registered trademark of HarperCollins Christian Publishing, Inc.

Tommy Nelson titles may be purchased in bulk for educational, business, fund-raising, or sales promotional use. For information, please email SpecialMarkets@ThomasNelson.com.

ISBN 978-1-4002-3336-6 (audiobook)
ISBN 978-1-4002-3333-5 (eBook)
ISBN 978-1-4002-3334-2 (HC)

Library of Congress Cataloging-in-Publication Data is on file.

Written by Dale Earnhardt Jr. with Caryn Rivadeneira

Illustrated by Ela Smietanka

Printed in Korea

22 23 24 25 SAM 6 5 4 3 2 1

Mfr: SAM / Seoul, Korea / August 2022 / PO #12083245

To our girls, Isla and Nicole.

Buster rolled into the garage.

"Why the long hood, buddy?" Coach Hog asked. "Practice wasn't *that* bad."

Buster sighed. Practice was worse than bad. It was exactly what Buster worried it would be: a disaster!

PUNCHY MOTORSPORTS
03
PUNCHY MOTORSPORTS
8
8
2

Ever since Hotfoot Racing went out of business and left him without a team to race for, Buster worried about everything. And even after Punchy Motorsports rescued him, his worries stuck around.

Buster worried about learning his way around his new garage.

He worried about making friends.

He worried about losing.

He worried about the *nervous rumblies* in his undercarriage that **squeeeaked** out his exhaust pipe. How embarrassing!

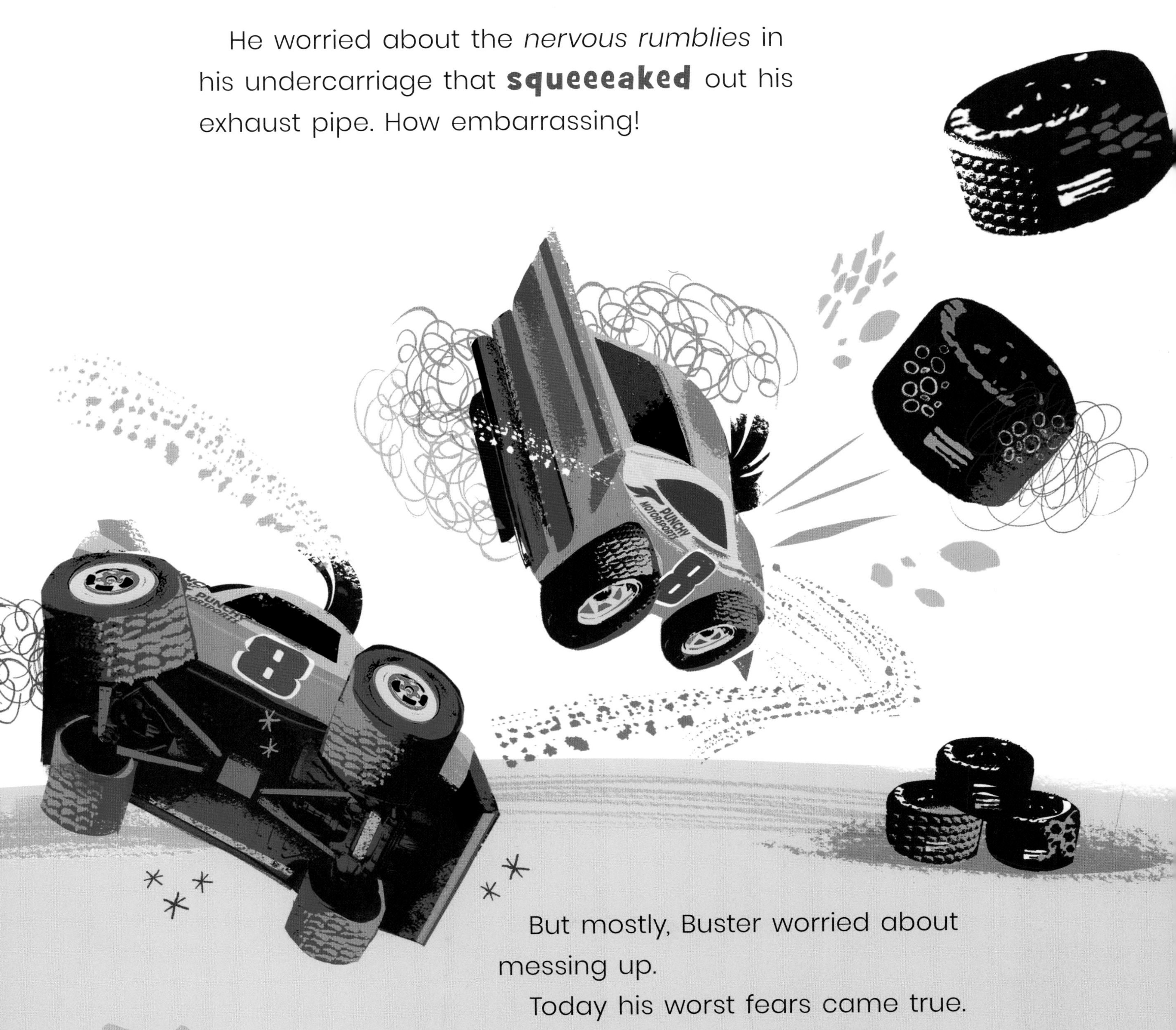

But mostly, Buster worried about messing up.

Today his worst fears came true. He messed up again and again . . .

CRASH!

CLANG!

BANG!

. . . and again.

"Your new guy sure lives up to his name," Scuff yelled over from Sneak Attack Racing's stall. "Buster **busts** everything!"

"Listen, kid, our mistakes can help *shape* us," Jimmy Jam said, admiring the hood dent that made his fans swoon. "Take Coach Hog's famous technique, the Bumper Thumper. He'd send cars spinning by thumping them with his bumper. It all began as a mess-up!"

"Snort-snort! Sure did," Coach Hog said. "That mistake became my signature move."

"Believe it or not, kid," Jimmy Jam said, "even *I* used to get nervous—until I learned Coach Hog's secret."

"Secret?" Buster leaned in.

"Take your mind off *your* worries by helping somebody with *theirs*! Snort-snort!" Coach Hog said.

"Really?" Buster said.

"Really!" Click said. "And remember, we race against each other, but we're teammates! We've got your fender."

"Sure do, kid," Jimmy Jam said with a wink. "Like I always say: It'll be A-OK on race day!"

"I hope so," Buster muttered.

Race day was tomorrow!

Ladies and gentlemen, start your engines!
The flagman climbed into the flag stand.
The crowd went wild.
Click **revved**. Scuff **sneered**.
Jimmy Jam flashed his smile at Buster
and winked. "It'll be A-OK . . ."
"On race day," Buster whispered.
If only Buster's nervous rumblies believed that.

BLURRRRP!
PUNCHY MOTORSPORTS
PUNCHY MOTORSPORTS
PUNCHY MOTORSPORTS

7
8
PUNCHY MOTORSPORTS
18
9
33
5
PUNCHY MOTORSPORTS

The green flag **whooshed** back and forth.

The cars roared to life. Around and around they sped.

Jimmy Jam **zipped** and **dashed** his way to the front of the pack. Buster **zoomed** behind—in Jimmy Jam's draft.

Maybe I can slingshot past him, Buster thought.

As he planned the tricky move, Buster's nose began to twitch.

What's that smell? he wondered.

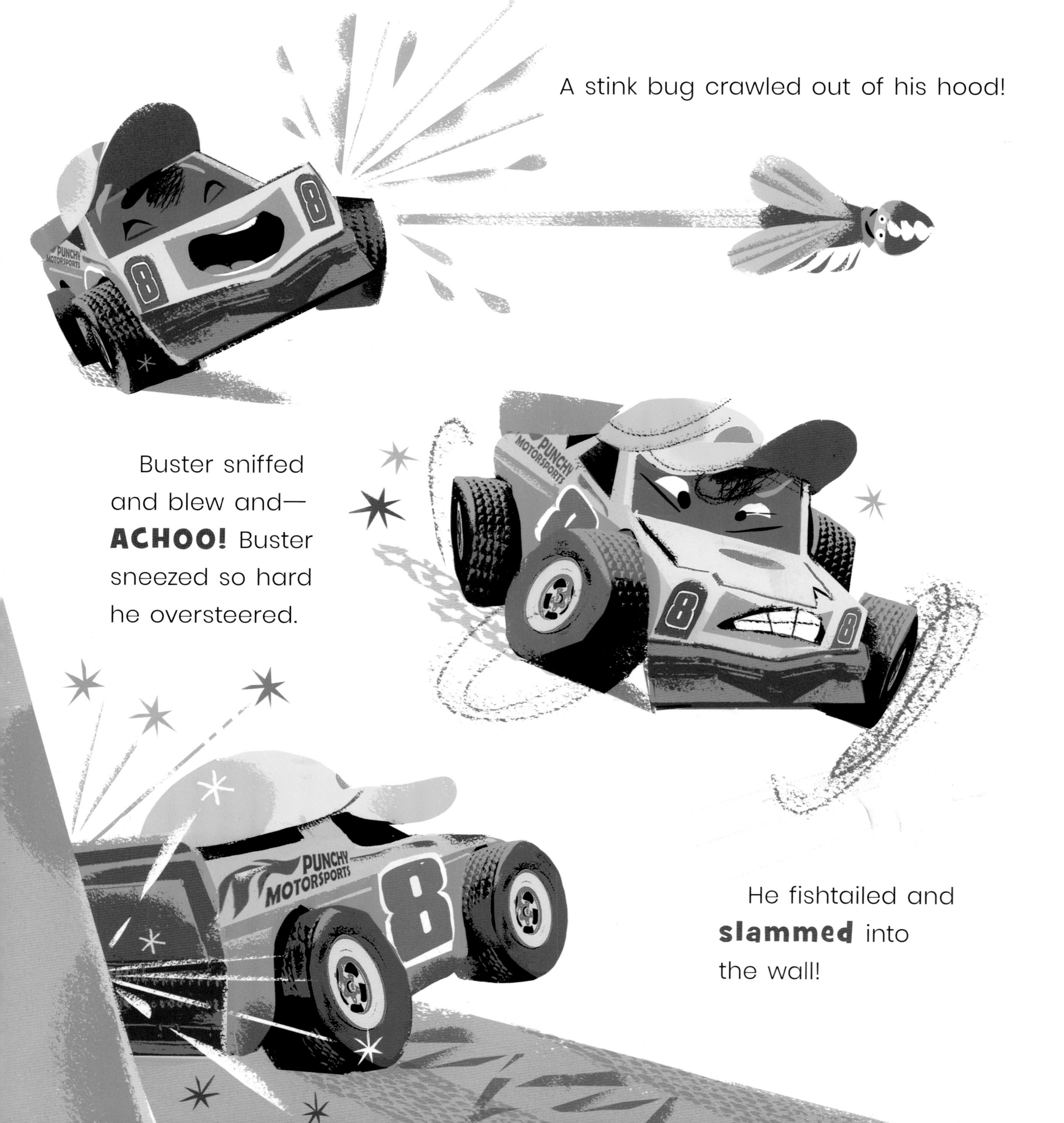

A stink bug crawled out of his hood!

Buster sniffed and blew and—**ACHOO!** Buster sneezed so hard he oversteered.

He fishtailed and **slammed** into the wall!

"Another Buster blunder," laughed Scuff as he peeled ahead.

Oh no, thought Buster. *I really do bust everything!*

Buster wished he could sneak back to Punchy Motorsports's garage and never, *ever* come out. Instead, he slunk onto pit road with his tires and pride deflated.

But Buster had the best pit crew in the garage, and with a few quick repairs, it was A-OK! Then they changed his tires with a **zip-zip** of the air gun and filled his gas tank with a loud **glug-glug-glug**.

Coach Hog tapped his fender and said, "Good to go! Remember, listen to your spotter about road conditi—"

But Buster wasn't listening. He was too focused on outrunning his nervous rumblies.

Buster's radio **crackled** and **hissed** as he peeled onto the track.

"... ooge ... ash ... ahead," his spotter said.

What did she say?

Buster coughed and his eyes watered. Smoke had filled the track. Cars had spun out and piled up.

Oh! Buster thought. *Huge crash ahead!*

He plugged his nose and blinked his eyes.

Buster **zigged**. He **zagged**—right past Jimmy Jam, who was caught in the crash.

"It'll be A-OK . . ." Jimmy Jam yelled.

"On race day!" Buster yelled back.

Buster **zoomed** up behind Click and Scuff.

He pulled left, then right. At each move, Scuff cut him off.

As they neared the finish line—**POW!**—Click's tire blew. Bits of tire rained onto the cars.

Scuff veered hard and scraped the wall.

Click spun across the track—and right toward Buster!

We're gonna crash! Buster thought.

Buster's nervous rumblies roared.

No time to worry. Click needed his help, and Buster had an idea.

If Coach Hog's Bumper Thumper could send a car spinning, Buster thought, *maybe it could stop one too.*

Buster had to try. After all, they were a team. They had his fender, and he had theirs!

Buster revved his engine, turned his tires, and—**BAM!**

He thumped Click's bumper—just as Scuff appeared in Buster's side mirror.

"Oh no!" Buster gasped. He couldn't let Scuff and Sneak Attack Racing win.

Click stopped spinning only a few feet from the finish line! She was down one tire—and Scuff was **zooming** up fast.

As Scuff was about to pass them, Buster gave Click's bumper an extra thump. **BAM!**

It worked! Click crossed the finish line just seconds before Scuff!

Cheers erupted throughout the speedway. *Excited* rumblies filled Buster's undercarriage as the checkered flag whooshed.

Click won!

Cameras flashed. Confetti sparkled through the air.

Reporters rushed to ask Click about her latest victory. She shrugged.

"Ask Buster," Click said, waving him over to victory lane. "His quick thinking saved us both. Who knew Coach Hog's Bumper Thumper could work in reverse?"

Buster rolled over to Click. A photographer snapped a picture of Click, her trophy, and Buster at her side.

"We call it the *Thumper Bumper*," Coach Hog told a reporter. "Get it? The *reverse* Bumper Thumper? Snort-snort."

Jimmy Jam winked at Buster. "Told you it'd be A-OK, kid! Nothing to worry about. Glad you're on the team."

Buster smiled. He still had things to worry about. But now he knew the secret to overcoming his nervous rumblies. Helping Click had helped him *and* saved the race for Punchy Motorsports.

Buster may not have won, but his team did! And he still made it to victory lane.

RACING D

AIR GUN: A tool that tightens and loosens lug nuts (which keep the tires on)

DRAFT: A pocket of air that has less wind resistance behind a fast-moving car

FISHTAIL: The out-of-control swing of a car's rear end from side to side

FLAGMAN: The person on top of the flag stand who waves the flags

PIT CREW: People who service a race car during a race

PIT ROAD: The slow lane off the racetrack where cars make their pit stops

PIT STALL: Where the pit crew changes tires and gives the cars fuel